The Night Shimmy

THE NIGHT SHIMMY
A PICTURE CORGI BOOK 0 552 54936 3

Published in Great Britain by Picture Corgi Books,
an imprint of Random House Children's Books

First published in Great Britain by Julia MacRae 1991
Red Fox edition published 1993
Picture Corgi edition published 2003

1 3 5 7 9 10 8 6 4 2

Picture Corgi Books are published by Random House Children's Books,
61–63 Uxbridge Road, London W5 5SA,
a division of The Random House Group Ltd,
in Australia by Random House Australia (Pty) Ltd,
20 Alfred Street, Milsons Point, Sydney, NSW 2061, Australia,
in New Zealand by Random House New Zealand Ltd,
18 Poland Road, Glenfield, Auckland 10, New Zealand,
and in South Africa by Random House (Pty) Ltd,
Endulini, 5A Jubilee Road, Parktown 2193, South Africa

THE RANDOM HOUSE GROUP Limited Reg. No. 954009
www.kidsatrandomhouse.co.uk

A CIP catalogue record for this book is available from the British Library.

Printed in Hong Kong

THE NIGHT SHIMMY

GWENN STRAUSS & ANTHONY BROWNE

PICTURE CORGI

Eric did not like to talk.
Other children didn't understand why.
They called him "Dumb Eric".
They teased him with silly questions:
"What's the matter? Cat got your tongue?"
Grown-ups asked him if he was shy.
But Eric didn't answer

He just didn't like talking.

And anyway he didn't have to talk
because his secret friend, the Night Shimmy, spoke for him.
The Night Shimmy explained why Eric couldn't
eat his peas, or why he didn't need a bath.

The Night Shimmy always chose the best stories
to read before Eric went to sleep.
And if Eric had frightening lizard dreams,
the Night Shimmy shooed their flicking tongues away.

When Eric's father asked, "What would you like for breakfast?"
the Night Shimmy said, "Porridge, please.

The Night Shimmy could be invisible, see in the dark,
and speak in the language of Shimmy, which only Eric and the
Night Shimmy knew. The Night Shimmy was also an expert spy.
He could hear the smallest sounds... a creak on the stairs

...or the crack of a kite in the sky.
Marcia was playing in the park.
She caught them spying.
She didn't care that Eric was quiet.
She didn't ask him silly questions, or try to
make him talk, or call him "Dumb Eric".
Even the Night Shimmy didn't have to say a word.

Marcia and Eric climbed the apple tree and
swung around like monkeys.
Eric made gorilla noises.

They flew Marcia's parrot.
It hung in the sky until the sky lost almost all its colour.
Then Marcia said goodnight, and Eric ran all the way home.

When he woke up the Night Shimmy was not there.
Eric searched under the covers, in drawers, in cupboards,
and in all of their secret hide-outs.
His mother asked, "What's the matter, dear?

Eric stayed in bed until
his father called three times.
All day long he thumped and kicked things.

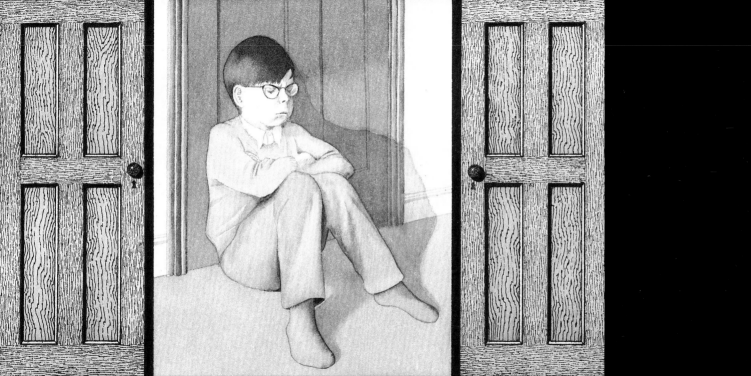

All on his own he climbed to the very top and freed the kite.

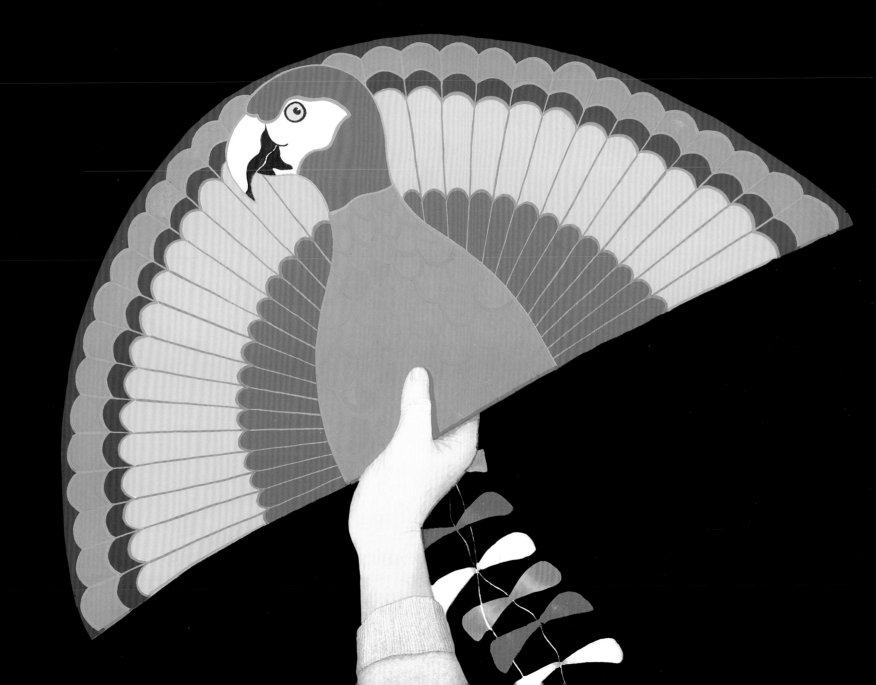

They began to talk.
Eric found he had many things to say.

When a breeze came up, they flew Marcia's kite,
until the first stars came out. They made silent wishes.
Then Eric said, "Goodnight."

And the Night Shimmy waved.